# Different Like Me

Lisa DeFini Lohmann

Illustrated by Richa Kinra

Outskirts Press, Inc.
http://www.outskirtspress.com

Paperback ISBN: 978-1-9772-0448-6
Hardback ISBN: 978-1-9772-0703-6

Illustrated by Richa Kinra.
Illustrations © 2020 Outskirts Press, Inc. All rights reserved - used with permission.

Outskirts Press and the "OP" logo are trademarks belonging to Outskirts Press, Inc.

PRINTED IN THE UNITED STATES OF AMERICA

Experience life's ups and downs
with the one and only
Wilson Highstep

This book is dedicated to my loving husband for
his unwavering support with this book, to my
most wonderful dad for always having loved me
unconditionally, and to Wilson Highstep for
filling my heart with such joy!

# Table of Contents

# CHAPTER ONE
# LIFE IN PEEPERS PET STORE

I t was just another typical weekend at Peepers Pet Store. Lines of people walked by, people of all ages and sizes, all looking at the puppies in their pens. Everyone was saying the same kind of things: "Look how cute that beagle is." "Oh, how precious is that little fluffy poodle." "Mom, Dad, I want that one. Please can we take him home? Please?"

Wilson did his best to look cute, but for some reason no one ever asked for him. He nuzzled goodbye to his friends one by one as they got picked and headed off to their new homes. Squeals of delight came from the little children as they walked out the door cradling their new pups in their arms. The adults hugged each other and smiled so wide their faces lit up with excitement while they walked out with their new additions. When a puppy found a new home, it was always a wonderful moment in the store. You could just feel the happiness in the air.

The weekends went that way for the first few months of Wilson's life at Peepers Pet Store. Every Sunday night Wilson told himself not to worry, as surely he would be picked the next weekend. After all, things were not that bad at the pet store. When he wasn't trying to look cute for the customers, he spent most of his days playing with his friends. He actually liked the big special pen that he shared with his furry friends. It was right in the front window of the store and had the best views of the outside, with all the wonderful things in life that were waiting for him someday. He imagined playing on the soft green grass or smelling a pretty flower as he walked by it. But for now, the best part of being in his special pen was the way the sun shone in late every afternoon, warmed his little belly, and lulled him into a restful nap. Yes indeed, life was pretty good.

Mr. Peepers was a happy-go-lucky kind of man. He had a big puffy mass of white hair that Wilson thought seemed to be in a constant state of motion on the top of the man's head, even when Mr. Peepers was standing still. His hair reminded Wilson of the big white clouds that floated gently in the sky outside his window. Mr. Peepers whistled little tunes and talked to the puppies all day while he went about his work in the store.

For a while though, Mr. Peepers had been sad because his business had not been doing well. Then Mr. Peepers got these new friends, partners, Wilson heard him say, and now everything seemed back to normal, because Mr. Peepers was whistling again.

On weekdays things were different in the store. Few customers came in, but there was plenty of other activity going on. Police Officer Rick walked by every day as he patrolled the neighborhood. He would gently tap on the glass to get the puppies' attention. Wilson loved the way the police officer's big brown moustache jumped around when he smiled at them and told them to behave.

Mr. Mike, the mailman, brought the mail almost every day. He always stayed longer than he should when he delivered the mail. After he placed the mail on the counter for Mr. Peepers, he'd bend into the pen until the pups could reach his face. He'd let them cover his face with the best puppy licks of love they could manage. He always laughed and would say, "Oh you can all do better than that." Then he would bend in closer for more kisses.

Mr. Tony, the delivery man, always sneaked treats to the pups as he wheeled supplies into the store. He gave a hardy laugh, and then whispered to them not to tell Mr. Peepers who gave them the treats. Wilson loved the way Mr. Tony's large belly shook when he laughed. Wilson often wondered how many people treats it took to get a belly so big.

Yes, Wilson decided, his pen was the best pen to be in.

Every Monday Mr. Peepers's partners brought in more new pups. Wilson was always friendly to the new pups, and he did his best to jump around with enthusiasm to welcome them to his special pen. The partners bringing the pups in seemed to make a big deal out of who got to be with Wilson in the front pen and who went to the pens in the rest of the store. Surly, he thought, it was a sign of how special he was, because the partners always left him there.

Monday was also bath day. One by one the pups got to walk through the store to the back area where the tub was located. Wilson never liked the walk to get there, as the rest of the pens in the store were not as nice as his. They were stacked one on top of another and they were small. The air was not as fresh, the lighting was dim, and the pups were separated from each other, making snuggling and playing impossible. He wondered if the afternoon sun ever made it back there to warm their bellies. All the pups back there seemed sad. They did not jump around to greet him as he passed by. He was not sure why, but something about that whole area made Wilson feel uneasy.

## CHAPTER TWO
## WHY DON'T THEY LIKE ME?

The weeks continued to pass with the same routine, except on Mondays when the new pups came in, the partners now began pointing at Wilson. He noticed he had grown much larger than the rest of his friends in the special pen. He even tried to hide the length of his body under the paper bedding in the pen to make himself look smaller. He began to worry and knew he had to do something, and soon, to be chosen by a new family.

The next day while warming his belly in the sun, Wilson thought about his problem and decided he simply needed to learn some cool tricks to attract more families to himself. That night, and for the rest of the week, after Mr. Peepers turned off all the lights and left, Wilson stayed up late and practiced his best tricks by moonlight. Tricks such as spinning around and catching his tail, dancing on only two feet, and smiling sweetly for what he hoped would be his new family. Who could resist him now, he wondered. By the time he was finished practicing on Friday night, Wilson had all his new moves down pat and was ready to impress everyone the next day. He snuggled down real low in the bedding to cover his eyes from the early morning sunrise so he could get some extra sleep. He was, after all, very tired from all the practicing.

Well, Wilson's plan didn't work out exactly as he had hoped. He was so tired that he slept the whole day away and missed all the new families that came in on Saturday. By the time he woke up, the crowds were gone and it was dinner time in the pet store. He felt a little nervous, and he knew he had to work extra hard on Sunday to make up for lost time.

He woke up bright and early Sunday morning all excited, believing that today would be the day he would be chosen for a new home. When the first family came in, he did all his tricks, faster than ever, but he was puzzled at their reactions. Why, they laughed at him! He thought that reaction was strange, but surely the next family will be impressed and want to pick him. But the same thing happened with the next family too. In fact they laughed even harder and pointed fingers at him. I don't understand this, thought Wilson. Why are they pointing and laughing at me?

Wilson continued to try his hardest all day, doing his tricks for all the people who entered the pet store, but their reactions were all the same. One by one, he sadly said good bye to his small furry friends as their forever families chose them. With his nose pressed against the front glass window of his pen, he watched his friends all walk down the street with their new families until they were out of sight. By the end of the day, he was once again all by himself in the pen. When he finally went to bed that night he felt scared and very much alone.

## CHAPTER THREE
## MISS BEANY'S BATHS

The next day started out much like every other Monday, but when Wilson walked to the rear of the store for his bath, the rest of the pups lifted their heads and nodded to him.

Hmmm, that's odd, he thought, but he quickly forgot about his troubles and the strange behavior of the pups during his bath. He really liked bath time, including Miss Beany, who gave the best baths in the world. Warm, sudsy water; a gentle shampoo massage; being dried with a warm, sweet-smelling towel; and a vigorous brushing to fluff him at the end all contributed to Miss Beany's perfect baths. The entire time Miss Beany sang to him and told him stories of what it was like when she was young. Her sweet brown eyes shone with happiness and love when she spoke, just like the families leaving the store with their new puppies. When he was all dry, Miss Beany would put her hands on her hips and exclaim how handsome he looked. She would then make a big fuss about what color bowtie to put on him. In the end she always decided on the red plaid one, saying it was her favorite, which Wilson really liked. She then gently picked up Wilson and whispered how God had made him extra special, before she gave him hugs and kisses while she carried him back to his special pen in the front. Yes, he loved his time with Miss Beany as much as he loved warming his belly in the afternoon sunshine.

The end of this particular Monday's bath routine was very different, though. On his way back to his pen, he heard loud voices up front and saw the partners who were bringing in the new pups arguing with Mr. Peepers. When they saw Wilson in Miss Beany's arms, they pointed at him, and their voices grew even louder. Wilson knew something was very wrong and snuggled down tightly in Miss Beany's arms, trying to hide. Finally, the partners calmed down and left.

When it was all over, Mr. Peepers took Wilson from Miss Beany and hugged him. "I'm real sorry, little guy," he said. "If I don't put you in the back, my partners will not bring in any more new pups, and I will go out of business. But don't worry, you are very special, and I'm sure you will have a forever family of your own one day real soon."

When Mr. Peepers turned with Wilson to walk to the back room, Wilson caught a glimpse of Miss Beany, who was still standing by the front pen, as if frozen to the spot. Her face looked sad. Her sweet eyes were no longer smiling but instead were streaming tears. "Oh no," thought Wilson. "What's happening to me?"

## CHAPTER FOUR
## IS THAT REALLY ME?

Once Mr. Peepers put Wilson in his new pen, Wilson suddenly realized why all the other pups had looked up and nodded at him this morning. It was their sad way of trying to welcome him, as if they knew what was going to happen to him after his bath with Miss Beany that morning. His new pen was small and cold, with barely enough room for him to stretch out. The bedding was hard and scratchy against his skin. There was a pen above him and two pens below him, with other stacks of pens just like his filling the room. There was such a feeling of sadness in the air. Wilson was tired from the events of the day, so he decided just to go to sleep. He curled up as best he could against the side of the cold metal pen. He could still smell the sweet shampoo and conditioner on his body that Miss Beany used on him earlier. It somehow comforted him as he tried to forget the day's events and fall asleep.

In the morning, he was awakened by a tiny ray of sunshine beaming down on his face. When he first opened his eyes, he almost forgot what had happened the day before and where he was now. He rolled on his back, trying to get the sunshine to warm his belly, but no matter how he squirmed to change position, the pen was not big enough for him to do so. When he was rolling back over, he noticed how the sun had lit up the metal wall on one side of his pen. When he looked closer, he saw his reflection for the very first time. Oh no, he thought, I'm not handsome at all like Miss Beany tells me. He looked nothing like any of the other pups he had ever seen. There must be something wrong with the wall, he thought. Perhaps it's just dirty.

Wilson used his tail to try to wipe the wall clean, but it was no use. The reflection he saw was still the same. He stared more closely at his image and did not like what he saw. His bottom teeth stuck way out from his lips, and his ears were large and dragged on the bottom of the pen. His body was way too long, as if it did not know when to stop growing. His front legs were shorter than his rear legs, as if he was standing facing down hill, but he knew he wasn't. Even his tail was strange. It was so fuzzy it looked like a big messy feather duster. And his hair! What was with this crazy curly hair all messed up on the top of his head, he thought. He tried to pat it down like he remembered Miss Beany doing, but it was no use. It simply sprang back up, bouncing all over his head like a bunch of wild springs. Even Miss Beany's favorite red plaid bowtie was all wrinkled and twisted sideways now.

The more he stared at all the things he disliked about himself, the more upset he became and then began to notice something very strange happening with his ears. They slowly rose until they stood straight out sideways, like the wings of an airplane. Oh, why can't I look like all the other cute puppies with small ears, normal hair and teeth, he thought. The more upset he got, the more his ears continued to lift upwards, beyond his control. Oh boy, I am doomed, he thought. No wonder why the weekend people always laughed at me. I'm so ugly, no one is ever going to want me. And with that thought, he could no longer hold back his tears.

## CHAPTER FIVE
## THE BACK ROOM

After a few minutes, Wilson's crying woke up everyone in the entire back room; but instead of them telling him to stop, all the other puppies joined in with him. After a while Wilson realized that he was not the only one crying and he stopped to listen. He heard big howls and small ones, and the dogs were all saying the same thing. They were all scared too. Wilson felt bad, because he remembered how he used to hear their howls when he lived in the nice pen in the front, but he had never stopped playing to listen to what they were saying. He always thought they were just acting poorly and misbehaving.

Eventually the other puppies began to quiet down, and one by one they stopped crying. The puppy in the pen on top of him spoke first. "Hello, my name is Max. I don't know how long I have been here anymore, but every time someone new joins us, we all have a good cry together, to just let the sadness out of our systems."

"Does it help?" Wilson asked.

"No, not really," Max chuckled. "But we do it anyway as our kind of sad welcome. You see, none of us were ever chosen by a family for one reason or another. They told me I was going to grow up and be mean and bite people."

"Mean? Bite? Why did they say those things about you? That's so hurtful," Wilson exclaimed.

Max replied, "I'm not mean. I'm just big for my age. You know, a bit chunky." And with that Max began to cry and howl again.

Wilson thought Max must be rather large, as he noticed that his pen was rocking back and forth with each of Max's howls. "Max, Max," Wilson called to him. "It's going to be okay. Please don't cry."

"How do you know? You just got here," Max replied.

"Well I don't know exactly," said Wilson "but I do know at least we have each other to talk to, right?"

Max stopped crying. He slowly slid his paw down through the bars of his pen as far as he could, to try to reach Wilson.

At first Wilson was nervous seeing how large Max's paw was compared to his own and pulled away; but he decided to be brave and slowly reached up to touch Max's paw. Wow, it feels just like my own paw, Wilson thought.

"Thanks, little buddy," Max said. "No one ever wanted to be my friend before."

After that, one by one, all the other pups introduced themselves to Wilson. By the time they were all finished, there was almost an air of happiness in the back room.

Max must have fallen back to sleep, because a loud snore came from his pen. Strangely, Wilson found it comforting as he listened to his new friend Max breathing in and out. Wilson circled around in his pen a few times in an attempt to find a comfy spot. He settled back down, thinking all the while how his new life was going to be in the back of the store with Max and the rest of his new friends.

## CHAPTER SIX
## MY NEW FRIENDS

Wilson dozed off for a while, before he was startled by the sound of Mr. Charlie opening his pen door. Mr. Charlie was the caretaker of all the puppies in the back room. When Wilson lived up front he used to hear Mr. Charlie's big voice and often wondered what a person who sounded like that would look like. Well, his big voice certainly fit his big body. He was big, very big, so big and tall that Wilson was amazed by how fast Mr. Charlie could move between the tight spaces of the pens and not knock any of them over. His hands were so large they barely fit in the door of Wilson's pen, yet they tenderly lifted Wilson out of his cage and up to Mr. Charlie's chest in one swift move. When Wilson looked up at Mr. Charlie, he saw that his big brown eyes looked warm and loving, like Miss Beany's.

Mr. Charlie saw the puzzled look on Wilson's face and said, "Hey little m-m-m-man, you're n-n-n-new back here, r-r-r-right? Well d-d-d-don't you w-w-w-worry, Mr. Ch-Ch-Ch-Charlie will take g-g-g-good care of you."

By the time Mr. Charlie had said all of that, he had scooped three more pups up out of their cages and held them all safely in his big arms. Wilson had never heard anyone speak like that before, yet Mr. Charlie seemed really nice. Hmmm, why doesn't he talk like the rest of us Wilson wondered.

Wilson was amazed at how safe he felt in Mr. Charlie's arms along with all the other pups.

"You g-g-g-guys stay r-r-r-right here. I have to g-g-g-get big M-M-M-Max," he laughed. Mr. Charlie put them all down in a large pen on the floor and then headed swiftly back to the stack of pens to get Max.

Wilson could hear Mr. Charlie talking in his unique way the entire time, even as his big voice trailed off when he headed back to the pens. As soon as his voice faded away, it started its way back.

He was laughing and saying, "M-M M-Max, old b-b-b-boy, you sure g-g-g-give Mr. Ch-Ch-Charlie a work out. Can't hold any other pups with you any m-m-m-more, you are g-g-g-getting so b-b-b-big."

Wilson was trying his best to see into the dim

light of the back room where Mr. Charlie was. He was a bit nervous, but excited as well, knowing he was only minutes away from seeing his new friend Max for the first time. Everything was happening so fast this morning. It was different from anything he had ever experienced. Before he even had the chance to finish his thought, Mr. Charlie plopped Max down right next to him.

"You g-g-g-guys stay put and b-b-b-behave while I g-g-g-get your b-b-b-breakfast," Mr. Charlie said as he headed away.

Wilson felt his eyes grow wide as he slowly looked up to see Max's huge face hanging right above his. He could feel his ears rising up and tried to pull them back down. Max's teeth were huge and his body was large and muscular. Wilson was glad Mr. Charlie's eyesight was good, as Max surely would have crushed him if he had landed on top of him. Wilson felt like running in the other direction until Max spoke.

"Wilson, my little buddy, is that you?"

Still nervous and overwhelmed at Max's size, all Wilson could say was, "Yup."

Max's mouth full of scary teeth quickly turned into the biggest smile Wilson had ever seen. Instantly, Wilson knew it was ok. The two dogs then jumped and played and nuzzled each other joyfully. For a minute Wilson forgot his sadness and where he was. When they finally slowed down, Wilson was amazed at how someone so different from him could make him so happy just by being his friend. He had never thought to play with anyone that looked like Max. It turned out they were not that different from one another after all.

## CHAPTER SEVEN
# The Great Outdoors

After the pups in the backroom ate the breakfast that Mr. Charlie brought to them, he took them outside to a big fenced in yard to get some fresh air.

At last I'm finally going outside, Wilson thought, just like all the pups that go to homes. At first the spring breeze scared Wilson, because he had never felt anything like it before; but Max explained to him that the wind was a good thing, even though he could not see it. Even so it made Wilson's ears perk up and flap around in strange ways that Wilson did not like. The minute his feet touched the grass for the first time, Wilson quickly forgot all about his ears. The grass was cool and soft, and tickled his toes. Still not sure of this new sensation under his feet, Wilson walked around slowly at first, lifting his legs up high, prancing around like a parade horse.

Officer Rick was making his rounds at that same time and noticed Wilson outside. He laughed and called out, "Hey, Wilson. Mr. Wilson Highstep, don't worry, you won't sink in. You just keep doing that fancy high-stepping foot work of yours, and you will be fine."

Wilson did not hear him because he had started to roll in the grass. He was mesmerized by the way it felt and enjoyed its delightful smell.

"Hey, go easy there, little buddy," Max said to Wilson. "Try to stay clean. We don't get many baths in the back room, and no one likes a smelly dog."

Wilson laughed, but continued poking around, smelling all the flowers, and trees that he had never been able to get close to before.

The two dogs spent the rest of afternoon chasing each other around and playing all sorts of doggie games in the sunshine and wonderful spring breeze.

After a while the sun started to go down and the air got a bit cold outside. Wilson was thankful that Mr. Charlie showed up in the nick of time and took them all back inside to eat dinner.

Wilson noticed how Max ate his small bowl of food so quickly.

Max saw Wilson looking at him and said, "If there is any extra food, Mr. Charlie gives it to me, because he knows I am always hungry."

There was no extra food that night, though,

and Wilson could hear Max's stomach growling. "Here," Wilson said, "take the rest of mine." He pushed his bowl closer to Max. "I'm full."

Quite shocked over Wilson's gesture, Max said, "Thanks, little buddy. No one has ever shared with me before."

Soon the dogs were all put back in their pens and the lights were turned off. Wilson was so exhausted from all his running around outside that he decided to go right to sleep. As he was trying to get comfortable, he heard his tummy growling but was still glad he had shared his dinner with Max. "Good night, Max."

"Good night, little buddy," Max replied.

Wilson tucked his head down low to sleep, but when he got a whiff of himself, he laughed. "P.U.," he thought, "I'd better listen to Max so I don't become a big smelly mess."

# CHAPTER EIGHT
# A NEW LIFE

And so as those first days went by, Wilson's routine was pretty much the same every day, except for when he discovered a new flower to smell or a new sight to see. Wilson listened closely to Max and learned a lot from him about life outside the pet store. There were so many creatures in the great outdoors, like the butterflies, ants, and mice that Max taught him about. But Wilson's favorites were the birds; how they flew around so easily with the breeze that now no longer scared Wilson. They simply tilted their wings to go up or down, left or right, and then they landed so gracefully. His other favorite creatures were the squirrels. He was amazed by how they could jump from tree to tree with ease, using their long tails for balance. He laughed at how carefully they would dig and search for acorns to hide under the big oak tree in the yard like it was a race. The big oak tree was the perfect home for all the little creatures that Wilson was learning about in the yard. Even though its large branches and leaves now blocked out most of the sunshine, there was just enough sunshine left for him to warm his belly with after rolling on his back on the grass. As Wilson lie there almost falling asleep with the sunshine streaming down and the gentle breeze blowing on his face, he thought about how he no longer saw Max as being different, but just as his new best friend.

# Meet the real Wilson Highstep

41

# CHAPTER NINE
## AN OLD LIFE

oon, Wilson almost forgot about being sad and about missing his old life in the front of the store.

Then one day when he and Max were outside, he heard Mike the mailman's voice. He suddenly stopped playing with Max and turned his head toward the voice. "Mr. Mike, Mr. Mike, I'm over here," he barked, but Mr. Mike did not hear him.

Then he heard another familiar voice. It was Mr. Tony unloading his truck to bring in his weekly round of supplies to the pet store. Once again, Wilson called out but it was no use, they did not hear him. He felt his eyes filling up with tears and quickly remembered missing all of his old friends.

Suddenly, Max was by his side and lay right down. "Hop on little buddy," he said and stood up with Wilson balancing carefully on his back till he lifted him up high enough to be able to see through the small knothole in the fence.

Wilson could now clearly see his two old

friends talking and laughing. He yelled again to them but it was no use, his voice did not reach them. The more he got upset and yelled to them, the more his ears rose up. Sadly he hung his head down and wiped away a tear running down his cheek. Max slowly lowered his body back down so Wilson could climb off and said, "Oh boy, don't be sad little buddy, you still have me."

"I know," Wilson replied, "but I miss my… hey wait a minute, why didn't you ever show me this hole to the outside world before?" Wilson asked while jumping down off of Max's back.

Max hung his head down very low and whispered in a very little voice, "Because I was afraid I'd lose you, my only friend. You see no one has ever wanted to be my friend before. Just because, well you know, I'm a bit husky, so I don't look cute like them."

"You don't look like them?" Wilson questioned. "Well I don't look like them either. I'm different too."

With that, they both stopped and just looked at each other. "Hmmm," Wilson said, "I don't get it. We're both different, which I always thought was a bad thing, but we're both good friends… so maybe being different is ok?" Before Max could answer, Mr. Charlie called them all in for dinner, so now Max had his mind on more important things…food!

## CHAPTER TEN
## THE DAY IT ALL CHANGED

Over the next few weeks, the weather began to turn cooler and Mr. Charlie could not leave them outside to play as long. The leaves on the trees started to turn pretty colors and then fall to the ground. It was fun to run around on them with all the crunching sounds under his paws, but once he was back inside, Wilson could not stop thinking about his old life and friends. He did not ask Max to lift him up to the peephole again because he didn't want to make Max feel bad, but deep down inside he would have liked to. Even the breeze that once cooled him on hot summer days now made him cold. Max would see him shiver and come close beside him to warm his little buddy. He would tuck Wilson in a corner and block the wind with his own body.

"See little buddy," he would say with a laugh, "all that food you share with me makes me a bigger, better blanket for you."

Wilson would smile, but he just didn't feel much like laughing these days.

And then, one day it all changed. There was a big storm blowing in that made the wind blow extra fierce that day. Mr. Charlie had just called them all to go back inside early when it happened. They all started to run for the door, and in the blink of an eye a big gust of wind whipped around the corner, over the fence and swirled around in the yard like an invisible enemy.

This is no regular breeze Wilson thought. He was trying his hardest to keep up with Max but the wind was getting to him. He was running as hard as he could, but he felt like he was getting nowhere. The wind kept holding him back. Max looked over his shoulder and noticed Wilson was falling behind. He yelled to him, "Hurry up, little buddy. I don't like the feeling of this wind."

Wilson felt his ears rising up with fright knowing he was trying his hardest, but he still couldn't keep up. He yelled to Max for help, but the wind was howling so loudly that Max could not hear him. Wilson felt his tail swaying back and forth with the wind. His ears were straight out sideways like the wings of a airplane. Even his bowtie was moving, twirling around in a circle like a little propeller. And then it happened… his feet lifted right off the ground. "Hey, what's happening?"

he yelled out. Max saw what was going on and started to bark wildly for Mr. Charlie to help. He tried his hardest to jump up and grab Wilson but it was no use. Before Max or Mr. Charlie could get to him, Wilson floated above their reach, higher and higher in the air. Wilson tried everything he could to get back down to the ground, but it was no use, the wind had a mind of its own and a big adventure in store for Wilson.

## CHAPTER ELEVEN

# FLY, WILSON, FLY

Now this was certainly no graceful first flight. Wilson was spiraling all over the place in the air, like a balloon suddenly losing all of its air. He twisted and turned with the rhythm of the wind going up, down and even sideways. But soon he calmed down and realized if he tilted his ears in a certain way he could pretty much straighten out, just like the birds he had watched. He used his tail to give him more balance, just like he watched the squirrels do. Even his bowtie was helpful circling swiftly with a smooth humming rhythm that gave him more control. Okay, I think I can kind of do this now Wilson thought. He watched the ground below getting further and further away. Max and Mr. Charlie's voices could barely be heard anymore. Higher and higher he was going and slowly the little fenced in yard that was once home for him began to look as small as a postage stamp. Even the big oak tree looked like a small bush from up there. He saw people walking in and out of Peepers Pet Store who looked very small now as he passed in and out of the clouds.

Little by little Wilson was able to better control his movements and actually began to enjoy his newfound ability. As he swooped down towards Max and Mr. Charlie, he could hear them calling to him to come back down, but now he was having too much fun. He graced them with a few moves he now had down pat. Then he headed back up towards the clouds calling out in a loud voice not to worry, he'd be back down before it got dark out. He was not only having fun flying, but he was amazed by all the beautiful sights he could see from so high up. As he was heading back up, he wondered how much higher up he'd have to fly to see where God lived. Surely someone as wonderful as God would live on the very top where it was the most beautiful, he thought.

When Wilson passed through the other side of the cloud he saw a big forest and decided he'd swoop down to take a closer look. He got down lower until he was just above the tops of the trees when he heard people yelling something. Oh, they must be calling to me Wilson thought, but then he noticed that no one was looking up at him. They were all walking in one direction, like they were looking for something, and yelling out someone's name. Approaching the group of people, he spotted Officer Rick with his big flashlight.

In another area close by he saw a large group of children playing some kind of a game with a rather large ball. Looks like they're having lots of fun, Wilson thought, as they cheered each other on. But why were those other people yelling out and walking in another direction?

The sun was starting to go down now and Wilson knew it was time for him to head back, but he wanted to get just a little bit closer to hear what they were all saying. His curiosity was now getting the best of him.

# CHAPTER TWELVE
## UNEXPECTED LANDINGS

Everything was going just fine. Wilson tilted his head down, turned his ears in a bit, and angled his tail just so for a smooth descent, just like he had done when he had gotten down closer to Max and Mr. Charlie earlier.

Wilson was getting closer to the group of people now and could hear that they were yelling someone's name. It sounded like they were saying the girl's name, Ellie. He liked the name because it reminded him of a cute little girl with long brown hair and glasses who came to visit him every weekend at Mr. Peepers. She was just tall enough to see in to his special pen and would put her hand flat on the glass as if she was trying to reach in to pet him. Wilson would reach back with his paw and touch her hand by the glass, but she never said a word. The man she was with would lean down and softly say, "Keep your hands off the glass, Ellie. You don't want to scare him. Besides, I know you wouldn't want that puppy if you looked at him more closely." Then he would gently pull her along to see the next area of puppies in their pens. He wondered if Ellie missed him at all, not being in the special pen anymore.

Wilson was thinking more about Ellie now and was not paying attention to his flying. He did not notice that the wonderful breeze that was carrying him all this time was starting to slow down. All of a sudden he felt himself falling downward, spiraling uncontrollably, at a rapid speed. The trees and ground were coming closer and closer, faster and faster. Wilson braced himself for a crash landing, fearing the worse. Thankfully, he started to bounce off the tree branches, like a ping pong ball, bouncing his way downward, back and forth. A really big pile of branches on the ground softened his landing.

Once he finally landed, he took a moment to compose himself, then tried to shake his head free of all the leaves and twigs that were now lodged in his fur. Boy, what a mess I have made for myself now, he thought. How am I ever going to get back home? Slowly he stood up, and realizing it had grown dark, he began to get afraid.

# CHAPTER THIRTEEN
# NOT SO SCARY AFTER ALL

Wilson had never been afraid of the dark before. He actually felt very safe all tucked in at night at the pet store, but now he was hearing all sorts of strange sounds. Oh why didn't he listen to Max and Mr. Charlie and just go back down when he could have, he thought.

Just as he was almost done picking the twigs out of his fur, he heard something move not far from where he was standing. "Who's there?" he yelled out, but there was no reply. I must be hearing things, he thought to himself.

Wilson's eyes were starting to adjust to the darkness in the forest so that he could just barely see the area around him now. The moon was very bright in the sky, and it's light peeked gently through the pine tree's branches, making shadows on the ground. He started to move closer to an open spot where there was more moonlight when he heard the sound again. He turned quickly and ran in the other direction, deciding he did not want to meet whatever was making the sound. That's when it happened, he crashed head on into something warm and squishy. "Aghhhhhh get away from me," he yelled while trying to push himself away from it. But the warm squishy thing pushed back and yelled the same thing right back at him and then started to cry. Through the faint moonlight he could now see that it was a small person that he had run into, so he stepped closer to get a better look. Why it's just a little girl he said to himself. What's she doing out here, he wondered. He felt bad now that his yelling had made her cry. "I'm sorry for scaring you," Wilson said.

He waited for a reply but all he got were more sobs. "You know, the funny thing is you scared me too."

Finally, the little girl stopped crying and answered, "I did?" in a very small voice.

"Well, yes, I never expected to meet anyone here in the forest."

"Oh, then I'm sorry for scaring you too. I was just trying to make myself a bed from the branches to keep warm under when you came crashing down on my pile."

"Yes, I apologize about my bad landing. I was not paying attention like I should have been, then the wind died and suddenly I was not flying anymore."

"Flying? You are a dog. Dogs can't fly."

"Well, yes, I am a dog and I know I'm not supposed to be able to fly, but I have this thing with my ears when it gets windy."

As Wilson explained what happens with his ears when he gets excited, he thought there was something familiar about her but he could not place it. She had on cracked glasses and a dirty soccer outfit, but suddenly as she spoke he got it.

Taking a chance, he slowly moved closer to her, put his paw up to touch her and said, "Excuse me, but are you Ellie from Mr. Peepers Pet Store?"

She tried to adjust her glasses to see better but it was no use. Slowly, she raised her hand up to meet his paw and said, "Yes. Yes, I am. But who are you, and how do you know who I am?"

With that, Wilson touched his paw to her hand knowing that although she could not see him clearly, she would recognize their private hello from the pet store. When she felt his paw she said, "Is it really you, my dream dog from Peepers Pet Store?"

Well Wilson almost fell on the floor with joy hearing that he could possibly be anyone's dream dog. He was filled with happiness as he ran around her in a circle, nuzzling her legs and licking her hands. "Dream dog. I'm a dream dog," he kept saying the words over and over again.

Ellie began to laugh, feeling his excitement.

Soon they both calmed down and Wilson said, "Ellie, I know how I got here, but how did you get here?" Her laughter stopped quickly, and she became very sad as she told him her story.

# CHAPTER FOURTEEN
# Two Good Endings
# For Two Bad Decisions

It seemed that the group of children Wilson had flown over before were part of Ellie's soccer team that she played with every week.

Although Ellie enjoyed the exercise and playing outdoors, she told him that she didn't like the team because the other children made fun of her. When the parents were not around, the other children would tease her about wearing glasses and being so tall. They also called her all sorts of mean names because she was not as good of a player. This was all so hurtful to her.

She explained to Wilson that she never said anything to her dad, because she did not want to disappoint him. She was also a little nervous that he might not believe her. She just did not know what to do anymore. She was trying as hard as she could to be a good player, but she simply never got any better. She wanted so badly to just fit in and be "normal" like the other kids. She wanted to be friends with all of them and not stick out any more.

So today, when it was her turn to kick the ball, just as she was about to do so, someone behind her called out, just loudly enough for all the other children around her to hear. "Go ahead and miss it, four eyes, so we can replace you with two normal sized kids that can score a goal."

With that Ellie started crying again as she told Wilson what happened next. "The ball came at me so fast, and I was so upset after hearing those words that I missed the ball altogether, and it hit me right in the face. The whole team started to laugh. I just could not take it anymore, so I ran into the woods. I just kept running and running until I was as far away from them as I could get. I know now I should not have done that, but at the time it seemed like a good thing to do."

"I know what you mean," Wilson said as he thought about his bad idea that had landed him in the woods.

Ellie continued on and said, "When I finally stopped running, I realized my glasses were so badly cracked that I could barely see a foot in front of me, so I just sat down and cried till I had no more tears. I started to get cold and was trying to make a bed with the branches when you fell down on top of me."

Wilson started to laugh. Ellie got mad and said, "Well what's so funny about that?"

"Don't you see," said Wilson, "if it were not for the both of us making bad decisions, we never would have found each other."

"Well I guess you have a point," Ellie laughed. "Funny how things work out sometimes, huh? This started out to be my worst day ever, but now it's my best...except for being cold and lost that is."

"Yes, we have to work on getting you warm, and getting us out of here," Wilson said. "Besides your dad must be worried about you. I saw a group of people looking for you when I was still up in the air flying." With that, Wilson began tucking the softest branches he could find from the moonlit pile in to Ellie's clothes to warm her up. They both laughed saying what a cute tree she made.

## CHAPTER FIFTEEN
## A MOST UNUSUAL FLASHLIGHT

As they were laughing, Ellie saw sparks of light appear from Wilson's mouth. "Hey, wait a minute," she said, "Every time the moonlight hits your teeth it makes a beam of light come out of your mouth."

"Really?" Wilson looked up at the moon, smiled his best smile and saw what was happening. "We need light, but how are we going to…never mind, I know how. Ellie, give me your glasses please."

"But they are all broken."

"I know, but I think that if I hold them just like this in my mouth, smile my best smile and catch the moonlight just right I can…"

"Make a flashlight with the reflection of the moon's beams from off of my teeth," they both yelled with excitement.

"Boy, oh boy," Wilson said, "Whoever would have thought my crazy teeth could be so helpful?

"Or my glasses be so helpful? I love them now," Ellie cheered.

"But, Wilson, wait. I really can't see at all now."

"Hmm, let me think for a minute. I know… hold on to my tail. It's so fluffy that you can reach it easily and I will lead the way."

Why that's another one of my strange body parts that has turned out to be quite useful after all Wilson thought to himself.

So off they went to find their way out of the woods, a little girl that looked like a small tree, holding on tightly to the fluffy tail of a small dog with a most unusual flashlight! Wilson found himself taking slow, high steps and walking gently on the uncertain ground, just like the first time he had walked on grass. Yes, Wilson Highstep bravely walked into the darkness of the night knowing he had a very important little girl to protect. He tried to remember all the things that Max had taught him about being outside, as he wondered what his friends at the pet store were doing now.

## CHAPTER SIXTEEN
## LET'S GO HOME

As they walked slowly, Wilson would stop every now and then, sniff the air and try to catch the scent of the people he knew were looking for them, or hear the sound of their calls, but there was nothing.

After walking for a while, Ellie complained about being cold and tired, so Wilson stopped and guided her to a large rock nearby that she could rest on. He gently jumped on her shoulders and curled up around her neck, just like a scarf, to keep her warm. It made Ellie giggle because his fluffy tail kept tickling her nose. Wow, if I was not so long, I could never have fit around her shoulders he thought. Maybe it's not so bad being different after all. Maybe I am just right being me. Boy, God really knew what he was doing when he created me!

That thought quickly left his mind when suddenly he heard the faint sound of voices in the dark. "Ellie, listen up, do you hear that?"

"Hear what?" Ellie asked.

"The voices. They are calling your name."

"No. I don't hear anything."

"Yes, yes, I do. By me sitting up higher on you this way I can hear them now," Wilson said all excited. With that, he felt his ears starting to lift up and this time he was so happy they did as it allowed him to hear the exact direction the voices were coming from. "Boy, I really love my crazy ears now," he said out loud.

"And I really love my tall body now that it lets you hear better with those crazy ears." Ellie chimed in. They both laughed at just how wonderful it was to be different after all.

"Come on, let's go to your family," Wilson shouted. They quickly resumed their unique walking positions and walked as fast as they could toward the voices.

Soon the forest started to thin out, and Wilson could actually see people way down in the distance. He told Ellie what he was seeing, but then suddenly he stopped short.

"What's wrong, Wilson? Why did you stop?"

"Well, because I just realized that once you go back to them, we'll be separated, and I'll have to go back to Mr. Peepers and probably never see you again." He felt tears building up in his eyes at the very thought.

"No way. We will always be together now. Don't you worry about that. Why we bring out the best in each other. Isn't that what friends do? I get it now. You made me realize if it was not for all the things we don't like about ourselves, we never could have saved each other. Don't you see, we are perfect being different just the way we are. It's the way we were meant to be us."

"So being different is really a good thing then, right?" Wilson asked still not believing his luck.

"Absolutely, being different rules!" Ellie shouted with joy. "Just think of it like all the different flavors of ice cream, Wilson. You know like vanilla, chocolate, and strawberry. They are all delicious flavors, but in their own special and different way, just like they were created to be. One is not better than another. Just think about how boring the world would be if we were all alike...or if there was only one flavor of ice cream. God gave us all our very own special gifts to be different with."

"I believe you, Ellie, and I understand now. We are all one of a kind, just the way we are supposed to be. No one is better than another. Being different is a really good thing. Being different like me!"

With that, Ellie swooped Wilson up and gave him a big hug. All of a sudden he felt as special as he did when he was in Miss Beany's arms.

"Come on, Wilson. It's been a long day. Let's find my dad and go home now."

"Home...," Wilson repeated the word slowly out loud several times as he straightened his bowtie and patted his hair down in an attempt to look a bit better for when he would meet Ellie's family. "Home... I am finally going to my forever home, but wait... Ellie, grab my tail really tight please. I feel the wind starting up again, and I don't want to take any chances about flying away."

They both laughed out loud as they ran as fast as they could toward the people that Wilson heard in the distance.

# The End!

Experience life's ups and downs with Wilson,
one adventurous book at a time.
Here is a bit of what's to come next...

## CHAPTER ONE

# THE GIFT OF TWO FATHERS

Ellie held on tight to Wilson's tail as they ran closer to the crowd of people.

Although she still could not see much with her broken glasses, she trusted her little friend to keep her safe and kept up with his stride as they ran now.

The branches that Wilson had tucked into her clothes to keep her warm were coming loose now. They flew up in the air behind her leaving a trail. Even though everything in front of her was still very blurry, she ran with a newfound confidence like never before. Her head was up high, her posture straight and tall, with probably one of the biggest smiles she had ever worn on her face. It seemed like not only did Ellie leave the pine branches behind her as she ran, but all her sadness and insecurities as well. Soon enough, she too was able to hear the voices calling up ahead. The first one to spot them was Ellie's dad, Jimmy.

"It's Ellie... there she is! Look everyone she's safe. Oh thank God," he shouted.

Daddy Jimmy was a rather short man with blond hair. Wilson thought that Ellie must look like her mom, as she looked nothing like her dad. He rushed towards them so fast that Wilson jumped to the side for fear of not being seen in the dim lighting, and being run over by him. What Wilson forgot was that Ellie was holding on so tightly, that his sudden movement caused both of them to fall to the ground.

Ellie was not hurt as she landed on top of Wilson, but her dad could not see clearly in the darkness and thought a wild animal was trying to hurt her. He quickly grabbed a very large stick that was on the ground and raised it up to fight with this beast that now had his daughter.

TO BE CONTINUED.....................

You can write to the author at

Wilsonhighstep@yahoo.com

CPSIA information can be obtained
at www.ICGtesting.com
Printed in the USA
LVHW050044230720
661199LV00015B/838